양의

미래

UEA PUBLISHING PROJECT
NORWICH

KONG'S GARDEN

HWANG JUNGEUN

TRANSLATED BY JEON SEUNG-HEE

Kong's Garden
Hwang Jungeun

Translated from the Korean by
Jeon Seung-Hee

Published by
Strangers Press, Norwich, 2019
part of the UEA Publishing Project

Distributed by
NBN International
10 Thornbury Road
Plymouth PL6 7PP
t. +44 (0)1752 202301
e.cservs@nbninternational.com

Printed by
Swallowtail, Norwich

Series editors
Nathan Hamilton & Deborah Smith

Editorial assistance
Senica Maltese

Cover design and typesetting
Nigel Aono-Billson

Illustration and Design Copyright © Nigel Aono-Billson, 2019

ISBN: 978-1-911343-62-2

Yeoyu ——
new voices
Korea

the bookstore was located in an old, fairly dilapidated apartment complex in the basement of a detached commercial building, which, at only two stories high, looked like a simple, flat cake. Though spacious - the bookstore took up the entire basement floor - it didn't receive many customers in the beginning. It was tucked in an out-of-the-way area where the patronage had been in decline for years. The owner had propped an upright signboard next to the stairs leading down to the store and turned on all two hundred interior lights to announce its opening. At night, the light escaped through the stairway, making it clearly visible from afar. Passersby walking down the tree-lined street would notice the light, venture down to the basement, browse through the selection of books and buy a couple. Gradually, the store began to prosper.

I worked mostly as a cashier. When it wasn't crowded, I wore gloves and tidied up the bookshelves, checked the stock or mopped the floor. If I finished with all of that early, I went back to the counter and stared out the store entrance. There were clear days and gray days outside the six-foot-tall glass windowpanes. It wasn't a bad place to work. In fact, I liked working there, though I didn't realise it then. If I walked up the fan-shaped stairs to the ground level, I saw a cherry tree next to a streetlamp that seemed to spotlight the phone booth below. In spring, the cherry tree bloomed early. Around the time when its flowers began to fall, the petals would shine a silvery white. I could see it all from the counter. The flowers tumbled through the air, petal by petal, turning over on themselves dozens of times before reaching the ground. During that period, petals littered the stairs. When there was a gust of wind, they would whirl up from all the corners. The girl named Jinju disappeared on one of those days.

●

I've been working since I was a child. When I think of my middle school or high school days, I remember, above all, working somewhere - a hamburger chain, a KFC, a family restaurant, a book rental shop. At one point, I also posted fliers. On weekends, I fried shrimp for samples while standing on a supermarket corner.

I've always been working. I've realised this only recently. I don't feel like it is unfair and haven't regretted it. *That's just how it is,* I tell myself. *And that's that.* It was embarrassing for a moment, if I ran into classmates or peers at work, but it wasn't too bad and I quickly forgot about it. I could always forget about it.

Only once did I feel so embarrassed that I wanted to quit. I was sixteen and still in high school, working at a clothing store downtown during summer vacation. It was a cheap clothing store called *Roman or Roma*. The store's sign was written in italics and made of bronze. There was one customer who dropped by like clockwork every afternoon. She wore a formal suit and dragged an empty-looking suitcase. She would browse the store and then leave without buying anything. Once, I came over to help her. She seemed to be hesitating between a black sweater and a white one. When I told her that the white one was warm and suited her better, she looked straight at me, holding one sweater in each hand. *Why is white warm?* she asked. *White is a cold color, miss. It's a cold color. You never learned that in art class?*

My face flushed. I just stood there and stared, my face burning even hotter. I felt naked. It wasn't because I was embarrassed to be reminded of my ignorance or carelessness but because she'd called me, 'miss'. She hadn't called me 'student', as people usually did. I was so embarrassed I began tearing up. I stopped working at the store a few days later and never went back.

I went to a commercial high school. During my senior year, about half of the students were absent regularly since they'd already been employed by then. I'd also secured a job and I didn't go to school for most of my senior year. I'd achieved good grades in bookkeeping and thought that explained my swift employment.

But, in fact, my job had nothing to do with bookkeeping. I worked at the counter in a discount warehouse store, moving stuff here and there, scanning barcodes, notifying customers of prices, taking and sliding customers' credit cards and asking for their signatures. I worked ten hours a day. Every day, I pulled or pushed enormous amounts of merchandise and rushed an enormous number of customers through the store. Sometimes, customers came behind the counter and slapped me across my face over something trivial. But that didn't happen very often.

There weren't many memorable events while I worked there. Mostly, I remember my nerve-wracking efforts to get to the bus stop on time. The bus I commuted on came at long intervals and, if I missed one, I had to stand and wait thirty or forty minutes before the next one arrived. Since I didn't like to wait that long, I always ran to make sure I was on time. When I came home at night, I was so tired that I felt as though my hands and feet were melting, yet I still couldn't fall asleep. When I lay down and looked up at the ceiling, I felt a pain like the pressure of several adults standing on my chest. One day, I began coughing and it didn't stop. I was diagnosed with tuberculosis and had to quit. In fact, it was more like being fired. Five years had passed.

I stayed home, unable to work, fattening up until I fully recovered. Mother had been struggling with liver cancer for ten years and father was taking care of her and doing the chores around the house. He took care of me as tenderly as he did mother. He never said we were short on money or asked when I could begin to work again. Both of them were small, silent people and so our house was always quiet. As I lay there recovering, I sometimes felt as though my parents were in another room somewhere, holding their breaths. Then, without knowing it, I would also hold my breath.

During that period, I read a few books. Because I didn't want to buy new ones, I read what we had over and over again. Father's books were on the old bookshelves in the living room. I picked them out at random and read them in bed. Most often, the stories were written by a novelist who'd killed himself by jumping into a river when he was thirty-five. Two of his stories were included in an anthology of different short-story writers. One was written in the early stage of his career and the other around the time he committed suicide. The former was compact and powerful, but the latter was pretty stupid. In that one, the narrator was obsessed with something trivial and he became depressed and miserable. The story ended with lines like *I don't have strength to go on writing* and *I can't go on living like this.*

I can't remember any other details. Though I didn't enjoy reading it, I kept on. I think I wondered whether the writer hadn't been worried right before he killed himself. I also wondered what it would be like when I died. I thought I wouldn't want to be so stupid. I especially did not want to die and leave a stupid piece of writing behind. I didn't want to worry about it, whatever stupid thing I'd leave behind.

It took me almost a year to fully recover from tuberculosis. When I began to look for another job, I decided to take my commute into account. I saw a job ad for a bookstore that wasn't too far from my house. After inquiring about its precise location on the phone, I decided to walk over. The entrance was horribly messy because they were busy with preparations for the opening. After waiting there for about an hour, I was interviewed on the spot. I wasn't asked any difficult questions. Just, finally, *Can you work for long hours?* Yes, I answered. *OK, when can you begin?*

So the bookstore was a better place to work than my previous job. More than anything else, I liked that it was a bookstore. I didn't have to deal with customers demanding refunds for panties that had clearly already been worn. There was a cat there, too, who eventually gave birth to a litter in the shrubbery near the stairs.

Ho-jae named the kittens 'Siru', 'Injeol' and 'Kong'. Kong, the blackest and smallest among them, looked as if she were about to die. Ho-jae wiped the mucus off of Kong's eyes and rubbed her body with his thumb until the kitten became sufficiently warm, cradling her on his knee the whole time. He also unfolded an umbrella and hung it on a branch to protect the kittens from direct sunlight. After about five days, he lifted the umbrella and put a plastic box under the bushes.

I stood beside Ho-jae and watched him line the plastic box with a plastic sheet to prevent moisture from building up inside, drape old clothes over the entire construction, then place the kittens within. Finally, he covered it all with the umbrella. When Ho-jae and I left, the mother cat appeared out of the bushes, sniffed the area around the box and stepped inside.

The customers loved and cared for these cats like they were their own. Sometimes, children tried to hurt them, but Ho-jae would threaten them within an inch of

their lives. The bookstore owner eventually tried to
have the cats removed because he worried about angering
the children's parents. Ho-jae wouldn't budge and, apart
from this business with the cats, he was an excellent
employee. The cats were left alone in the garden.

Ho-jae left the bookstore before the cats did. He had
decided to finish his degree, which he'd given up on
years before, and began going to school again. He said
that he'd had the acute realisation that it would be a
hard life for a man who didn't have a B.A. to live in
a country where most people had at least one degree.
But he wouldn't tell me what had brought him to this
realisation. There must have been some incident, I
thought, and I felt a little sorry for him.
     After returning to school, Ho-jae studied hard.
Since he got out of the school library and I got out of
the bookstore at about the same time, we met at night.
Though neither of us had much money, we went to motels.
This didn't leave much for our actual dates. We saved on
food costs by sharing a hamburger or some other single
item and were often hungry during our hook ups. We'd be
even hungrier after. So we would take all the change out
of our pockets, spread it out on the bed or table in the
motel room and try to figure out what we could get to eat
with our collective scraps.
     Ho-jae was tall and had a habit of lying close to
the edge of the bed. When he lay straight and stretched
out his feet, he completely filled one side. It was
really strange how he never fell out of bed sleeping
like that. He really didn't move at all while he slept.

I once put a pillow on top of his belly for fun to see if it would stay in place. Sure enough, I found it right where I had left it and Ho-jae still sleeping when I woke the next morning.

While I lay next to him, I sometimes talked about my father. Father who took care of Mother without any complaints. Father who handled the affairs of our household without the slightest trace of machismo, who looked more like my grandmother than my father. My tiny-framed father.

I wish Mother would just die, Father too.

Had I really said that? I'm not sure which of the two sentences I'd said. If I hadn't said both of them, I must have said at least one of them. Then I told Ho-jae I'd never have a baby. He didn't ask me why.

After finishing his final semester without any problems, Ho-jae tried to find a job. It wasn't easy. The more screening and interviews he went through, the more dejected he became. He was employed once as an office clerk but quit within two months and became even more depressed. He said that he needed a lot more qualifications to land a good job. He said he didn't have anything that would make him stand out and that he felt this more and more acutely. He was rough in the motel bed, pushing my legs up abruptly and pressing down hard on top of my body. Under his unbearable weight, I studied his face carefully. Sometimes, we didn't use protection because Ho-jae insisted. But on those days, Ho-jae looked even more worried than me afterwards.

We had to restock the bookstore's inventory every three or four months. To do so, we had to erase the entire inventory that was already on the computer and input the new information on the books that remained on the shelves one by one. In addition to myself, three other workers had to labour overnight. Sometimes, this inventory work overlapped with my monthly spreadsheet task. One time, after this ordeal, I went to see Ho-jae in the middle of night with a thick bundle of receipts stuffed in my bag. Ho-jae was waiting for me at a motel. I had stayed up almost the entire night and so I dozed off while Ho-jae was still on top of me. He stopped and several beads of his sweat fell into my mouth. Surprised, I opened my eyes. I could feel a thin line of warmth spreading inside me. It was a terrifying feeling. I slapped Ho-jae's back with an open palm. *Don't.* He just stared down at me blankly.

He and I fought that night. Words we didn't completely mean poured out of our mouths and drew out even rougher words that surprised and hurt us even more. By the end, I was sobbing hysterically in the bathroom. Ho-jae sat on the corner of the bed and grimaced like a guilty child.

We continued to see each other for a while longer, then we just stopped. We fought in front of a movie theatre one evening. Ho-jae turned around and left me with the tickets and never came back. That was it.

I continued to work at the bookstore and took care of Ho-jae's cats. The three kittens all grew up and Siru and Injeol disappeared for a while, leaving only Kong at home. One day, Injeol returned, pregnant. Kong seemed to remember that Injeol was her sister. She sniffed around her and stayed next to her and, when Injeol's kittens were born, Kong was friendly towards them too.

There were always a few cats in the garden. They disappeared and returned to eat and then went away again. The female cats returned when they got pregnant. While the mothers and kittens went away and returned generation after generation, Ho-jae's umbrella remained open on top of the shrubs though its cloth was eventually torn and started to roll up over the ribbing. When it rained, I often stood near the entrance, listening to the raindrops bounce off the umbrella. *Where is Ho-jae now? Is he still sleeping in that odd way? Has he found a girlfriend who's able to understand his peculiarities?* Although Ho-jae had not done particularly ill by me, I thought he'd likely treat his next girlfriend better.

There were both clear and cloudy days behind the glass. The sunlight reached the bottom of the stairs only when the light was strongest. On both sides of the glass, it was sunny outside and shady inside. Though the bookstore lighting was almost too bright, the quality of the illumination was fundamentally different. I would look out more often on sunny days from within the store's pale and strident light.

I cannot remember exactly when but one afternoon while I was staring up at the stairs, burning yellow through the glass, I realised that I was exposed to sunlight less than thirty minutes a day. That I would stay here even when the sun was like this, and that time could fly by like this for me, I couldn't quite believe. I

thought I might not ever have a love affair again.
I could no longer imagine a chance for it.

There were four clerks who worked from morning until
evening in the bookstore and part-time clerks in
the mornings or afternoons. The owner posted hiring
information on internet forums. Kids who thought they
wouldn't be hired at better places came to work here -
kids who just stared blankly at things and who never did
anything other than what they were ordered to do; who,
when they were scolded for their mistakes, never lost
heart; who instead just stared back at you. Many of them
didn't show up the day after they got paid. Often, no
one could reach them later either.
     Jae-o was five years younger than me. A graduate
from a prestigious college, he was preparing for a civil
service examination. He said that he wanted to save
some money before he launched into exam preparation
full-time. He lived in an apartment near the bookstore
and began to work part-time in the mornings. After two
months, he began to work in the afternoons as well.
     He was a cheerful person, but conversations with
him always ended up getting strangely sidetracked.
Jae-o wasn't attentive to what other people said and
often said that he did things that he hadn't done, or
vice versa. And he frequently insisted he knew things
he didn't know, and vice versa as well. And then, when
it was proven that he hadn't known something, or that
he was wrong, he would just say, *Oh, I see,* as if he
had only been joking when he had insisted that he knew
something, or acted as if he had been right all along.

Jae-o also had the insensate tenacity to cut a thick plastic cord, which you could only cut with a special lever-shaped cutter, with a thin regular cutter by sawing at it hundreds of times. And he had a kind of numbness that would lead him to randomly touch a covered electrical wire as if nothing was precious or frightening to him. It was terrifying to watch him act like this every day.

One day, Jae-o came up and said, *Sister, do you know that the storeroom here is actually a passageway?*

There was an underground storeroom beneath the bookstore. A small door opened inward at the bookstore's western corner. Once through that door, stairs led further down. You might call it the underground floor of the basement.

This room was as large as the bookstore itself, which meant that it was as large as the entire building area. Thick pipes crossed each other geometrically on its high ceiling. The unpainted walls showed the building's cement finish. Jae-o claimed that this space was a part of an underground tunnel that connected every corner of the entire old, giant apartment complex. He said that he had heard about it from the building manager. There was a boarded wall in this underground space, beyond which was an enormous tunnel that connected every building in the apartment complex, according to Jae-o.

It's an underground tunnel so big that it can accommodate all the inhabitants of the apartment complex during war or similar situations. It's all connected, Jae-o informed me. *It's a shelter, you know, a shelter.*

He giggled.

   I couldn't understand why this was funny, why he would laugh. As I continued staring at him, Jae-o nodded as if he had understood something about me and then went back to his work.

There were drafts in the storeroom and it was hard to tell where they came from. They were cold and damp, suggesting that they probably contained a lot of mould. After Jae-o's claim, I assumed they must come from the tunnel. Sometimes, I even stood in front of the boarded wall and tried to listen in. The drafts really did seem to blow in from there. When I tapped the wall, I could hear a booming sound. It was loud and hollow enough that I could imagine there was indeed a tunnel behind the wall.

   After I started imagining what might be inside the tunnel, I no longer liked the storeroom. I hadn't really liked it before, but now I felt as if I was entering the bowels of some strange animal whenever I went downstairs - the bowels of a long, dark, enormous creature. During lunch hour, we went down to the storeroom, one by one, and sat on top of some of the boxes and ate. I sat facing the wall, as it felt better than having my back against it. During this period, I often had nightmares in which I would walk forever and ever in some endless dark space. If there was a turn or kink in the walkway, I thought I might be able to go out through it, but I kept going and going without ever encountering one. I walked and walked down a tunnel that seemed like the body of a huge millipede or snake. That was the only thing that happened in these dreams.

Jae-o worked for a year and half at the bookstore until one day, the day after payday, he just didn't show up. It was the beginning of the school semester, so we were all extremely busy. Anxious, the bookstore owner asked me to call him. I called and said, *Hello*, but he didn't respond. When I asked if he was going to come to work, he said, *Me? Why?*

He then demanded the bookstore owner pay him a retirement allowance. When the owner responded, *For a part-time employee?* Jae-o argued that it was his right guaranteed by the law and that he had a lot he could talk about concerning the bookstore's illegal bookkeeping and employment practices if the owner refused to pay up. According to Jae-o, the bookstore owner was violating the legal requirement that employers were all obligated to subscribe to four basic types of insurance (health, retirement, unemployment and accident) for their employees. The owner said that he felt betrayed. It was around this time the owner began to be careful around me and conduct some parts of his business in secret. He took books back from me and began managing them himself. And whenever he was unhappy about matters related to us he would mutter *ingratitude*.

I stayed in the bookstore and worked hard. Although not very often, I got raises occasionally which left me with some pocket money. Mother was still struggling with cancer and Father packed my lunch every morning, which included something boiled hard with soy sauce. Every day, I went down to the storeroom during lunchtime and ate, staring at the wall. That was how my days went by.

●

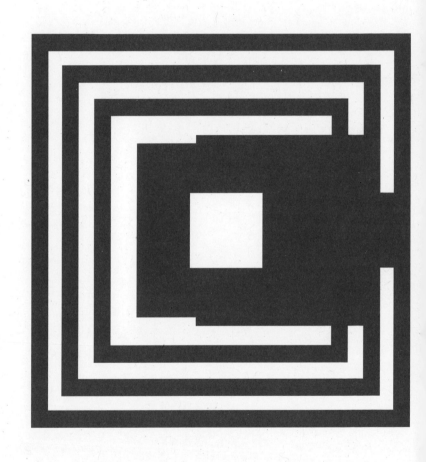

I saw the girl at the bookstore.

It was spring, a season that always seemed to drive us crazy with its beginning-of-the-semester frenzy. I was just standing around absentmindedly before the store closed and after I had sent away most of the customers who had rushed in at the same time. We sold cigarettes then. We displayed the cigarettes on locked shelves behind little glass doors by the counter. There were rules for selling them that I always followed. Since students frequented the bookstore, we only sold cigarettes to customers who could present IDs, except for those we knew well.

That night, a girl came to the store and stood in front of the counter and asked for two packs of cigarettes. She was wearing a school uniform with a ribbon around her neck and was holding paper money in her right hand. She was pretty and looked at me as if she was challenging me, though she also looked a little anxious. When I told her that I couldn't sell cigarettes to a minor, she said that she was on an errand. The adults were outside, she told me, and gestured. I turned my head and looked out to see two men standing near the phone booth. One of them was wearing a hat and looking in our direction.

Now, can you sell them to me? she asked me a little more forcefully.

When I told her, *Tell them to come down and buy them themselves,* she hesitated for a moment and then went out. I saw her walk up the stairs, approach the men, and talk to them. It seemed that she had told them what I'd said. Now the man wearing a hat was slowly walking down the stairs.

He looked smaller and thicker at the counter than he had outside. He was solidly built, wore a dark-brimmed hat and smelled of smoke. *Didn't that young girl ask for cigarettes just now?* he said politely. *I asked her to ask for me. Why didn't you sell her the cigarettes - you saw me outside?*

His eyes were blank and shaded by the brim of his hat, but I could see that they were blood-shot and yellow-white. When I said that he had to show me his ID if he wanted to buy cigarettes, he seemed to grin, rummaged through his pockets and took out his wallet. It was worn-out, leather. He took out a card that looked like his ID but didn't hand it to me, just held it in his hand and stared. *And why should I have to show you my personal information just to buy a few packs of cigarettes? Why should I, a full-grown man, have to do that? How can I trust you with my ID? Please, try to be a better cashier next time,* he said. Then he thrust his ID back into his pocket and strolled out of the bookstore.

The other man and the girl were waiting for him at the top of the stairs. They stood next to the phone booth and discussed something. In response to something the men said, the girl either nodded or shook her head. The men took their hands out of their pockets and touched the girl's head and the sides of her slender body. Every time they did this, the girl shrank back a little and laughed. Above the girl's head, flowers were falling like solid, dry snow.

I wondered what I should do. It was a strange scene. Indeed, very strange, even though there weren't that many things that made it so immediately. They were just standing together and talking. The men and the girl just looked so incongruous. I thought that they couldn't possibly know each other very well and felt uncomfortable about the whole thing. I tapped the counter with the tip of my finger and hesitated. Should I step outside now and ask her what was with them? Where and when had she met them? Did I have the right to ask her that? Should I just call the police? If so, what should I tell them? A girl was talking with some men? Was that enough to report to the police? Was it a crime? Even if it was a crime, was it my duty to report it? What should I do if my actions later put me in danger? What if I became the target of some plot to get back at me for my suspicions? After all, the bookstore would always be here and I would always work here.

Finally, I decided that I probably shouldn't get involved. It was too troublesome and the situation too ambiguous. It was much easier to just think that they were odd acquaintances. Who really knew? I wasn't naturally nosy enough to meddle in other people's business. I finished thinking about it before I had time to reflect on my decision, and I turned around and began to close the store, checking that day's sales data on the computer. When I looked up and outside at some point, they were already gone.

Afterwards, everyone kept asking me questions. I had never been such an important figure in my life. All kinds of people asked me again and again what I had seen. What were they wearing, what did they look like, what were

they doing, what was their manner of speaking, which
direction did they go in? I answered the questions
I could and said that I didn't know to the questions
I couldn't. The more important the questions were, the
more often I told them that I didn't know. What the men
looked like, which direction they had gone in. I was
summoned to the police station and shown a lot photos,
but I couldn't clearly identify them.

Who were they? Even now, when I think about that
question, I can only remember the man wearing the hat
and looking in my direction under the streetlamp. His
face under the brim of his hat, and even more shaded
because of the streetlamp that poured light just above
him, looked so different from - but, at the same time,
so similar to - the photos I was shown. After sweating
over the photos again and again, I pushed one over to
the policemen. They asked if I was sure, and I thought
it over and said that he looked the most similar, but I
wasn't entirely sure. I really didn't know much about the
incident. I learned from the police later that the name
of the girl who had disappeared was Jinju.

She had disappeared after purchasing a ticket to her
favorite pop singer's concert and her bag had been
found hidden deep inside the bookstore's garden at
the entrance of the apartment complex. One pair of
underwear, smeared with bodily fluids, was found at a
construction site near the apartment complex. It was
women's underwear, rolled up in ball and stuck between
some bricks. Her classmate, who was the last person
to see her before she disappeared, pointed to a bench

under a wisteria a hundred and fifty meters away from the bookstore as the place where they had parted. The police who came to search the area had eventually come to me. Since the incident involved a resident who had disappeared in an apartment complex, the news travelled fast. People visited the bookstore to check the location of the incident, or to ask whatever questions came to them. There were days when even random people yelled at me.

The girl disappeared here. You were the last person who saw her.

The heartless eyewitness.

An adult who did nothing to protect a child who needed protection.

That was who I became.

Then there was Jinju's mother. She came to the bookstore every day. She was a tiny old woman with dark skin, smaller than her teenage daughter with thin limbs and a small head. She looked like a person who had been shrunken, proportionally, or whose growth had been stunted. I thought perhaps she must have been the first child of a poor couple. Her pregnant mother must not have been able to eat well and then, on top of that, after she was born, as a child she must also not have been able to eat well. This was the image she stirred in me - and she must have given birth to Jinju when she was old.

Jinju's mother distributed fliers to passersby around the bookstore. There was always a bundle of them tucked at her side. After handing them out all over the area,

and travelling far to do so, she still dropped by the
bookstore every day. Every afternoon, she stood in
front of the counter and asked if I had seen the suspect
or if anybody resembling the suspect had dropped by the
bookstore that day, or if anyone had seen him nearby.
She then asked me what I had seen. She insisted that
I tell her exactly what I had seen. What the men looked
like. What Jinju was doing with them. How Jinju looked.
If she looked drunk. If she looked like she had been
beaten. If there were bruises on her face or wrists.
     If she looked like she had been threatened. If she
looked scared. If she was crying. Which direction they
had gone in. Which direction she had gone in. She asked
me the same questions over and over again. Then she
asked me what I was doing then. She always asked that
question last.

Jinju didn't show up, and she wasn't found. No calls,
no traces of her whereabouts. I thought about how there
really could have been an underground tunnel connected
to the storeroom in the space behind the wall that I
looked at every day during lunchtime. She hadn't been
found despite several thorough searches, but perhaps
she might have been down there. If it was an enormous
tunnel that stretched through the entire apartment
complex, as Jae-o had claimed, then maybe Jinju could
be hiding or hidden somewhere inside it. That's what
I thought. When I proposed to the commercial building
manager that we search down there, he stared at me, a
puzzled expression on his face. *What?* he said. He said
that there was nothing behind the wall. There was no

underground tunnel. He said that they had installed that wall a little way back because of the extensive mould on the original.

I returned to the bookstore confused. After finishing some cashier work, like any other day, I went down to the storeroom while all the other clerks and part-timers were having their lunch. I left my lunch on top of a box I used as a table and chair and searched the tool cabinet. Wires, flattened bond tubes, screws, nails, mousetrap tape, paint thinner containers, drivers, mould removers, sticks and tongs. I was looking for a hammer, but I couldn't find one. I kept on searching for it, knocking down and pushing away piles of things. I finally found a hammer covered with dried rags on a middle shelf. I stood in front of the wall with the hammer and looked at the corner, water and mould stains branching across its surface like vine patterns. I felt a draft blowing in from behind it. *The manager never knew about it. That's it. But there has to be a tunnel down here. Look, there's a draft. It's coming through the tunnel. Like this.* I could prove it. I could, just by swinging that hammer a few times. It would have been as easy as breaking eggshells.

And that was the reason I couldn't. To find the tunnel or to not find it: even today I wonder which of the two I'd be more afraid of. To find another dark hole behind the first hole in the wall or to discover another wall covered with mould, like a huge patch of sores. Which would be more horrifying? I didn't know and I probably won't ever know. I stood in front of the wall with the hammer in my hand for a while and then walked back to the box where I'd left my lunch. I laid the hammer down on the floor, drew my lunch box towards my knees and slowly began to eat.

After a short spring and summer, autumn approached rapidly. Jinju's mother continued to come to the bookstore. In the summer, she spread a straw mat near the stairs on which she propped Jinju's bag and photos. Sometimes, there were three photos and other times there were four. They were magnified, life-sized photos of her from the waist up and were of poor quality. She pasted them onto boards and wrapped them with plastic film. She stood two of them behind herself and one or two in front. Then she prostrated, small and round like a toad, and didn't move from there all afternoon. She grew older and you noticed the musk of her body when you were near her. A musk like a sack of old grain.

The bookstore owner, who had left her alone up until then, because of the sympathetic public opinion towards her, grew more nervous as time went by. One day, he told me to dissuade her from prostrating like that in front of the store. He told me to do this after saying that he felt sorry for her of course. I went upstairs as he'd ordered.

I noticed the bowls for the cats were empty. After taking the cat food bag out of its hiding place at the corner of the garden and filling the bowls to the brim, I walked up the rest of the flight. Jinju's mother was lying prostrate as usual and, as there was no shade over the spot where she lay, she had been exposed to the burning sun all afternoon. The shadow of the cherry tree might reach her around sundown. I looked down at her brown nape and narrow back.

Lady, what do you want?

Do you know how busy I am? Do you know how much work I do here? I can't ever come out and see the sun on beautiful days like this. I spend the entire day underground, never getting any sun, okay. So, why do you have to do this here? Why on earth here? Are you trying to put a curse on this store? Please just don't ask me what I was doing. When nobody cares about me, why should I care about others? Jinju, your daughter, who is she? Nobody. She's nobody to me.

While I looked down at her, unable to say any of that, my mouth feeling like it was sealed shut, a cicada began to sing. *Ooo-eee-ooo-eee.* The nape of my neck felt hot in the sun. I left her and began to walk along under the trees. My shins hurt because I wore my shoes with their heels folded.

I walked fast and I never returned.

○

Mother passed away four years ago. She died in the hospital room, her breaths ragged from abdominal dropsy. During her last moments, we quarreled bitterly with the hospital. They'd told us to take her home because they had run out of medical options. These days, I sometimes think that it might have been better for us to have taken her so that she could have faced death at home.

Father still lives in the same house. I think that

it finally became a normal life, as the house really only
has space enough for one person. He often says he'll
kill himself if he becomes ill. I just nod and listen
when he says that. I don't think he really will.

I left the house three years ago. When I packed my
bag, I packed a few of Father's books. Recently, I read
one of them, an essay collection by George Orwell. It
was about abject poverty - poverty even poorer than
that I had ever known. Recently, I've begun to think
about death a lot. Death from natural causes, illness
or accidents. I wonder if there could be any death more
miserable than dying when you're old, poor, ill and
without anyone to take care of you, as I'd read about in
Orwell's essays. Orwell said that no weapon humans had
ever invented could make someone more miserable than
dying a natural death in a situation like that.

Not coincidentally, he said that he wanted to die
suddenly and accidentally on the road rather than just
from being old. I wrote next to this sentence, *I agree,*
and then after pressing down hard on the paper with the
tip of my pencil a few times, I added, *If you don't have
relatives and you're poor, you'd better not have a kid.
You should die just poor and without anyone.* I closed
the book after that and thought about how the sentences
would still be there long after even I'd forgotten about
them. They'd be there ten years from now, and maybe a
hundred years after that.

There are many acacia trees in the neighbourhood where
I live now. The air has a freshness to it because
of all these trees not only on the hill behind the

neighbourhood, but also in the alleyways. Especially at night, you can smell them even from a bus stop that is fairly far away. When I make my way home along the alleyways after work, I often think of the old days. Some days, I think of Ho-jae. How he's doing. Did he get a good job? Did he find a girlfriend without too much trouble and finally have a kid? Siru, Injeol, Kong. Ho-jae's cats must have all died. What had happened to their offspring? Was the mother cat still giving birth to kittens? Were her kittens now giving birth to kittens?

I'm still doing the same sort of things. I still work and experience things that embarrass me, although not to the degree that they would bother me too much. If I feel too embarrassed to stand it any longer, then I quit and never come back. Of course, this doesn't happen very often. I hope that if I have to move to another neighbourhood there'll be a lot of acacia trees there too. Still, even if I end up in a neighbourhood without a single acacia tree, I'm sure I'll end up adjusting to it all pretty well.

How am I? I'm doing the same. Occasionally, very rarely, when the night gets too quiet, I search for articles about Jinju. An article saying that she'd finally been found somewhere. Even an article saying her remains had been found. I search for that article using all possible keywords I can think of.

I have told this story to no one.

●

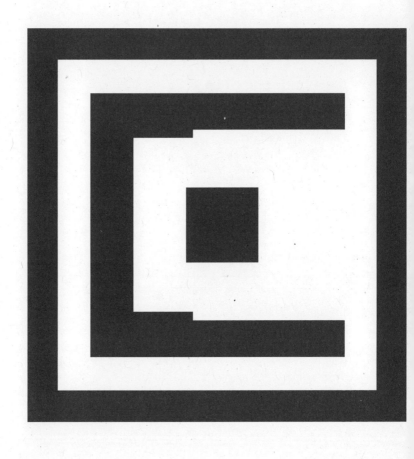

Kong's Garden

Yeoyu is a series of chapbooks showcasing the work of some of the most exciting writers working in Korean today, published by Strangers Press, part of the UEA Publishing Project.

Yeoyu is a unique collaboration between an international group of independent creative practitioners, with University of East Anglia, Norwich University of the Arts, the National Centre for Writing, and made possible by LTI Korea.

Yeoyu —
new voices
Korea